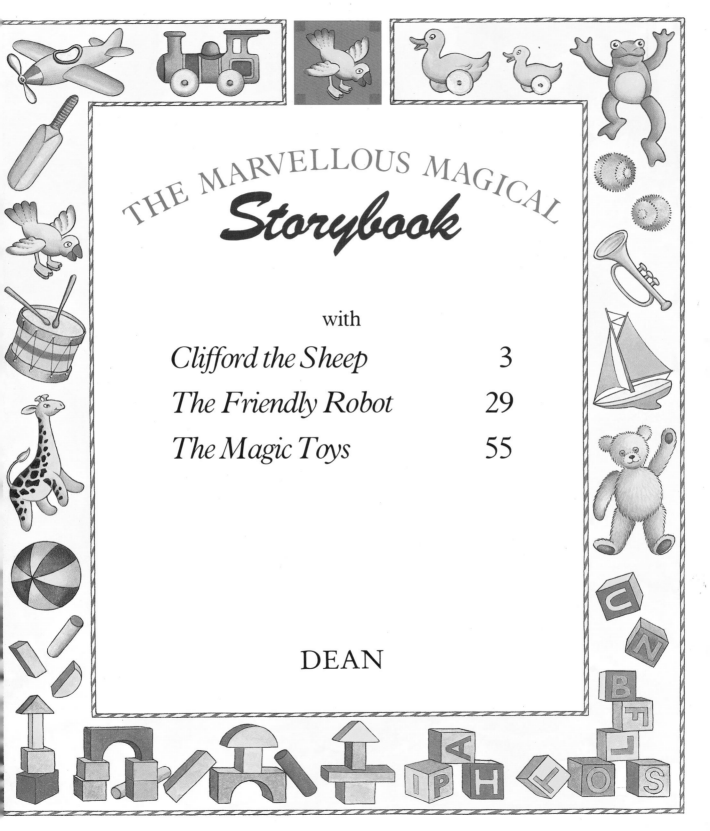

THE MARVELLOUS MAGICAL
Storybook

with

Clifford the Sheep   3

The Friendly Robot   29

The Magic Toys   55

DEAN

Clifford
The Sheep

SALLY SHERINGHAM

ILLUSTRATED BY PENNY IVES

Clifford was the happiest sheep in the world. He delivered newspapers and his job was to deliver the *Oakleaf Times* each morning. All the wild animals who lived near the farm looked forward to seeing him wobbling up their paths on his small red bicycle.

The animals always made sure that they had some blackcurrant tea brewing, and a pie or cake baking in the oven.

Clifford cleverly timed his visits. For example, he arrived at the Rabbits' house for tenses,

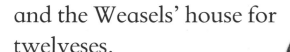

the Hedgehogs' house for elevenses,

and the Weasels' house for twelveses.

Then, he always went to the Spotted Woodpecker Inn for lunch. He loved his food and it was no wonder that he was getting rather plump!

The animals invited Clifford in every day because he kept them up to date with what everyone was doing. He was also an excellent story-teller, so when he was a bit short of news, he made up some stories. His favourite ones were about the wicked Fox Brothers who often visited the wood.

The Fox Brothers terrified the other animals. Once they really did steal some golden-feathered chickens from Mr Grey, the badger, who was the mayor. No one had seen Mr Grey smile or laugh since that awful night.

Clifford was such a chatterbox that it took him
all day to deliver the newspapers. He never arrived
at Mr Grey's house until suppertime. Mr Grey was
getting very cross because his paper was always
delivered late.

Then, one day, Mr Grey didn't get his paper at
all! Clifford had become so plump that he had got
stuck in someone's doorway! Every animal came
to help.

'One, two, three, *pull*!' shouted Graham Rat, and out popped Clifford, like a cork. But by then it was well past everyone's bedtime, and far too late to be delivering newspapers.

The next morning, Clifford was woken up by an angry knock on the door. It was Mr Grey. 'I have had enough of reading yesterday's news tomorrow or, in this case, reading no news at all,' he barked. 'I'm sorry, Clifford, but I shall have to give your job to somebody else. You not only talk too much, but you are clearly too fat and slow to deliver newspapers.'

So, Clifford was given a week's notice. His job was given to a stoat called Eric, who moved as fast as a roller-skater and only ever said 'Humph'.

Clifford's last day was very sad. All the animals made an extra-special fuss of him. This meant that he didn't arrive at Mr Grey's house till after suppertime. He pushed the last copy of the *Oakleaf Times* through the letter-box.

Suddenly, Clifford heard sinister laughter from inside the house. He knew that it couldn't have been Mr Grey laughing because Mr Grey never laughed. Nervously, he opened the front door and stepped inside.

There, before his eyes, were the wicked Fox Brothers. They were putting all Mr Grey's precious antiques into a sack. Then Clifford heard a muffled 'Help! Help!' coming from the grandfather clock, and sticking out of it was a grey stumpy tail. Mr Grey was shut inside the clock.

Trembling all over, Clifford crept towards the grandfather clock and unlocked it. Mr Grey slipped out and ran off to get help. Clifford was just tip-toeing after him, through the front door, when his heart sunk to his hooves.

Four sharp claws gripped his woolly shoulder! He nearly died of fright.

'Not so fast,' said one of the Foxes, and he slammed the door shut. Clifford was trapped!

'What a nice plump sheep,' said the other Fox.

'Er, I think I should warn you, gentlemen,' squeaked Clifford. 'Mr Grey has gone to the farmer for help.'

The Foxes laughed. 'Animals aren't friendly with humans,' they said.

'Mr Grey is,' Clifford lied. 'He and the farmer play cards and drink potato brandy together every night.' Clifford chatted on and on about the farmer, and because he was such a convincing story-teller, the Foxes believed him.

Suddenly, there was a crunch on the gravel.

'That'll be the farmer now,' said Clifford.
'You'd better run or your fur will end up as orange
hearth rugs.'

The Foxes didn't wait to hear more. They ran as fast as they could and as far as they could. In fact, they ran so far that they were never, ever seen again in the neighbourhood.

All the animals rushed through the door.
Clifford was safe and sound! What a brave, clever
sheep he was. Then Clifford told everyone how
he'd fooled the wicked Fox Brothers. It was the
first true story he'd ever told about them!

'Your story-telling has saved the day, Clifford,' said Mr Grey. 'I would like to apologize and to ask you to keep your job after all.' Then Mr Grey smiled for the first time since his golden-feathered chickens were stolen.

All the animals were happy, because Clifford was still going to deliver their papers and, of course, Clifford was happy too.

But what about Eric the Stoat? No one knew
how he felt, because all he said was 'Humph!'

THE FRIENDLY ROBOT

CAROLYN SLOAN

ILLUSTRATED BY JONATHAN LANGLEY

Paul stared at the heap of nuts and bolts and arms and legs on the kitchen table. 'Who is that?' he asked.

'It's a what, not a who,' said his father. 'Robot one-seven-nine is supposed to do the work of six men in the factory, but it doesn't.' He picked up the pieces and put the robot together.

'He looks friendly,' said Paul. 'Can I play with him for a while?'

'Not now,' said his mother. 'You have to tidy your bedroom. Take the thing with you. It's getting in my way.'

The muddle in Paul's room was knee-deep. Paul found a T-shirt in his bed and used it to polish the robot. It rattled happily and lights came on all over him. The robot had been programmed to put things in their proper places in a factory. Now it started to tidy Paul's bedroom.

'You *do* work,' said Paul happily. 'You work very well!'

The robot picked up Paul's clothes. It matched his socks, and sorted his soldiers.

Then it found Paul's construction set. It went wild and began to bolt and bang and build something HUGE!

'Hey! Slow down,' said Paul nervously. He pulled a lever on the robot's back and there was a whirring, coughing noise. Then the robot said, very clearly, 'I am making a friend.'

'You can talk!' said Paul excitedly. 'That's great! I never thought you'd be able to talk.'

'Of course I can talk,' said the robot, 'but no one has ever turned on my talking before. I suppose no one ever wanted to talk to me.'

'I want to,' said Paul. 'I'm Paul. Who are you?'

'I am one-seven-nine,' the robot said politely.

'That's just a number. You must have a name,' Paul replied. He thought for a moment and then said, 'I can give you a name. How about Robert-Robot, or Rob or Bob? That's a very good name.

You can be called Bob,' Paul decided happily.

'Bob-bob-bob-bob-bob-bob,' chattered the robot, and in his excitement he kept turning all kinds of bright colours, and he did a sort of dance. 'Bob-bob-bob-bob-bob. . .'

39

Bob looked at Paul's toys. He was introduced to
Teddy. Then he went back to the construction set.
'Can I make my friend now?' he asked. 'I've
always wanted to make a friend.'

'You can't build a friend with a kit,' Paul
explained gently. 'But cheer up! You've made a
friend already – me!'

Bob looked at Paul hopefully. He glided round him. 'Are you really my friend? Why are you such a small friend?'

'I'm getting bigger all the time,' said Paul, standing as tall as he could.

'I'm not getting bigger all the time,' said Bob.

'No. You came that size,' Paul explained. 'You have never been small.'

Suddenly Paul felt sorry for Bob. He had never been small, never been young, never had a family or friends. He had never had a home, only a factory, and he had never known how to have fun, only how to work. Paul decided to teach Bob how to have fun and play games, and Bob loved every second of it.

Paul's father was amazed to see them playing together. 'If that robot can play,' he said sternly, 'it can work,' and he took Bob back to the factory in a black dustbin bag.

Paul watched them go. 'You might let him walk with you,' he said sadly.

In the evening, Paul's father came home alone.

'Where's Bob, the robot?' asked Paul.

'It's in the back of the car,' said his father. 'It wouldn't work at the factory. It seemed to be sulking, just like you in a bad mood.'

Paul crept out to the car the next morning. He rescued Bob and put him together again. 'You'll have to come to school with me,' he said, 'or they'll send you to the dump and then you'll be gone for ever.'

At school, Bob flashed his best smiles to Paul's teacher. He sorted her books, played the piano and sang some robot-songs in numbers.

He played marbles with the children, painted a
picture of purple nuts and bolts and then cleaned
and tidied the classroom.

'You are clever,' laughed the teacher. 'I like having you here and the children have never been so good before!'

When Paul's father came to collect Paul, he was
amazed to see Bob learning how to spell. He saw
the teacher pat Bob's tinny shoulder, and heard her
say Bob was a good boy.

'Excuse me,' he said, 'but that is not a good *boy*.
It's robot one-seven-nine and it can come back to
the factory now, as it seems to be working again.'

'Oh no, I'm sorry,' said the teacher. 'Bob is much too young to go to work. He must come to school every day with Paul. He must have holidays and play games and go to bed early.'

Paul is bigger now. Bob is still the same size, and they are still the greatest of friends.

THE MAGIC
TOYS

PAMELA OLDFIELD

ILLUSTRATED BY KAREN MURRAY

One day, Miss Mabbs went downstairs into her toy shop. She spoke to all the toys as she always did. 'Good morning, elephant,' she said, 'and good morning bear.'

The elephant and the bear sat on the shelf and did not answer. The old lady smiled. 'Good morning, fairy doll. Did you sleep well?'

Again, there was no answer but Miss Mabbs did not expect one. She turned to the baby doll. 'How are you this morning?' she asked.

Miss Mabbs lived all alone and she thought of the toys as her family. 'Let's have some music, shall we?' she suggested cheerfully. She crossed to the little box which stood on the counter and lifted the lid. The box began to play a tune. It was a musical box.

Oranges and lemons
Say the bells of St Clements.

Just then, the postman came in with a letter.

Miss Mabbs did not receive letters very often so she was rather surprised.

She opened the envelope and began to read the letter aloud.

Dear Miss Mabbs,
The toy shop is very shabby and I think I will have to close it down. I will call tomorrow at nine o'clock sharp to have a look round and make up my mind.
Yours sincerely,
Benjamin Bundy,
Proprietor.

Poor Miss Mabbs was very upset. She stared round the little shop and saw, that it *was* very shabby. The windows needed cleaning and there were big cobwebs hanging from the ceiling. Paint was peeling off and the counter needed polishing.

Miss Mabbs shook her head. 'The whole shop
needs spring-cleaning,' she said. 'But I am too old
to do all that work. Oh dear! Whatever will
become of me?'

After Miss Mabbs had gone to bed that night, the little toy shop was very quiet and dark. The only light came through the shop window from the moon. Suddenly, a thin shaft of moonlight rested on the musical box and a strange thing happened.

The lid of the box opened all by itself and the box began to play *Oranges and Lemons*. Because it was a magic musical box, another strange thing happened. The fairy doll came to life! She yawned and stretched her arms as though waking up from a deep sleep. Then she flew round the shop and touched the other toys with her wand.

Soon, all the toys had come to life. The baby doll began to cry so they popped her into a wicker pram and rocked her from time to time. She stopped crying and listened happily to the musical box which played the tune again and again.

The rest of the toys listened to the fairy doll.

'We have to help poor Miss Mabbs,' she told them. 'We must smarten up the shop, otherwise Mr Bundy will close it down. He will throw Miss Mabbs out into the street and he will throw all of us out too.'

The toys were horrified.

'We must start at once,' cried the bear.

Soon they were working hard. The fairy doll
flew up to the ceiling and knocked down all the
cobwebs with her wand. The elephant fetched a
bucket of soapy water and washed the windows,
inside and out. The bear found a paint box and
touched up the walls with exactly the right colour.

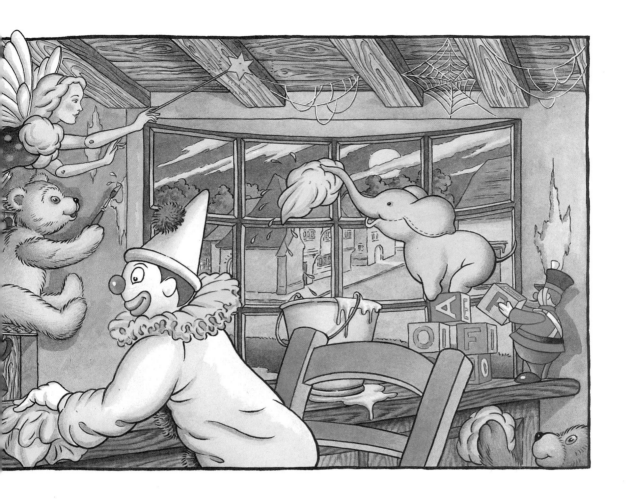

Then they swept the floor, polished the counter
and tidied and dusted the shelves. When at last
they had finished, the toy shop was spotlessly
clean, and as shiny as a new pin. The toys were
quite tired out but very happy.

Just then another moonbeam fell upon the musical box. Slowly, the lid began to close and the weary toys returned to their shelves. However, they forgot to move the baby doll, and she stayed in the pram.

The next morning, Miss Mabbs came down into her shop and found it spick and span. 'Whatever has happened?' she cried in astonishment. There was no answer. Then Miss Mabbs saw the baby doll. 'How on earth did you get there?' she asked. 'Something very strange has happened during the night, while I was asleep.'

At nine o'clock, sharp, the bell on the shop door jangled and in came Mr Bundy. He looked very puzzled. 'I don't understand it,' he spluttered. 'Last week, when I went past the shop, it was very shabby. Now it looks very smart.'

Miss Mabbs smiled sweetly at him. 'How very odd,' she said.

Mr Bundy glared at her. 'Well, I can't close
down such a smart toy shop,' he told her. 'I just
don't understand it at all.' He marched out of the
shop, looking very bewildered.

Miss Mabbs sat down behind the counter. She was very relieved. Her little toy shop was safe. She looked at the baby doll and wondered again what had been going on. 'You look very happy there, baby doll,' she said, rocking her gently. 'I think I'll leave you in the pram.'

Miss Mabbs opened the musical box and took out her knitting. Softly the music began again.

Oranges and lemons
Say the bells of St Clements.

First published in Great Britain by the Octopus
Publishing Group in three separate volumes

This edition published in 1993 by Dean,
an imprint of Reed Consumer Books Ltd
Michelin House, 81 Fulham Road, London SW3 6RB
and Auckland, Melbourne, Singapore and Toronto

ISBN 0 603 55123 8

Produced by Mandarin Offset
Printed and bound in Hong Kong